Teddy's Winter

This holiday story illustrates the value of friendship and the importance of sharing with friends.

Story by:
Ken Forsse

Illustrated by:
David High
Russell Hicks
Theresa Mazurek
Allyn Conley/Gorniak

I remember one morning not long ago, it was very cold when we woke up.

Page

Snowflakes are falling.

Grubby and I told Gimmick
about the wintertimes
in Rillonia.

The next few days were exciting. We were busy making gifts.

We were ready to start
delivering the gifts to
our friends.

The next morning we shared our gifts with each other.

O.K. Gimmick. It's your turn to open your presents.

Suddenly, there was a big knock on the door.

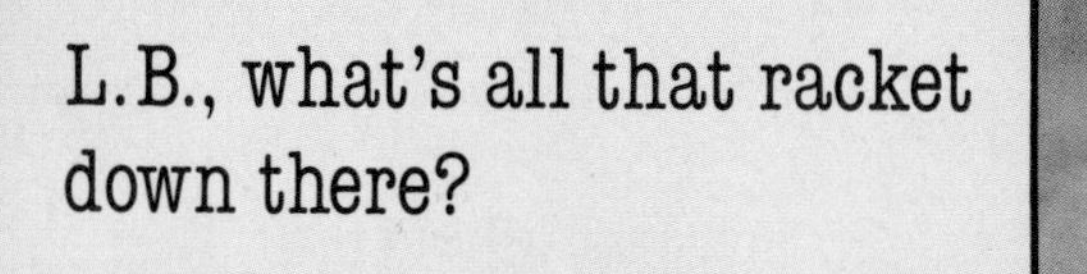
L.B., what's all that racket
down there?

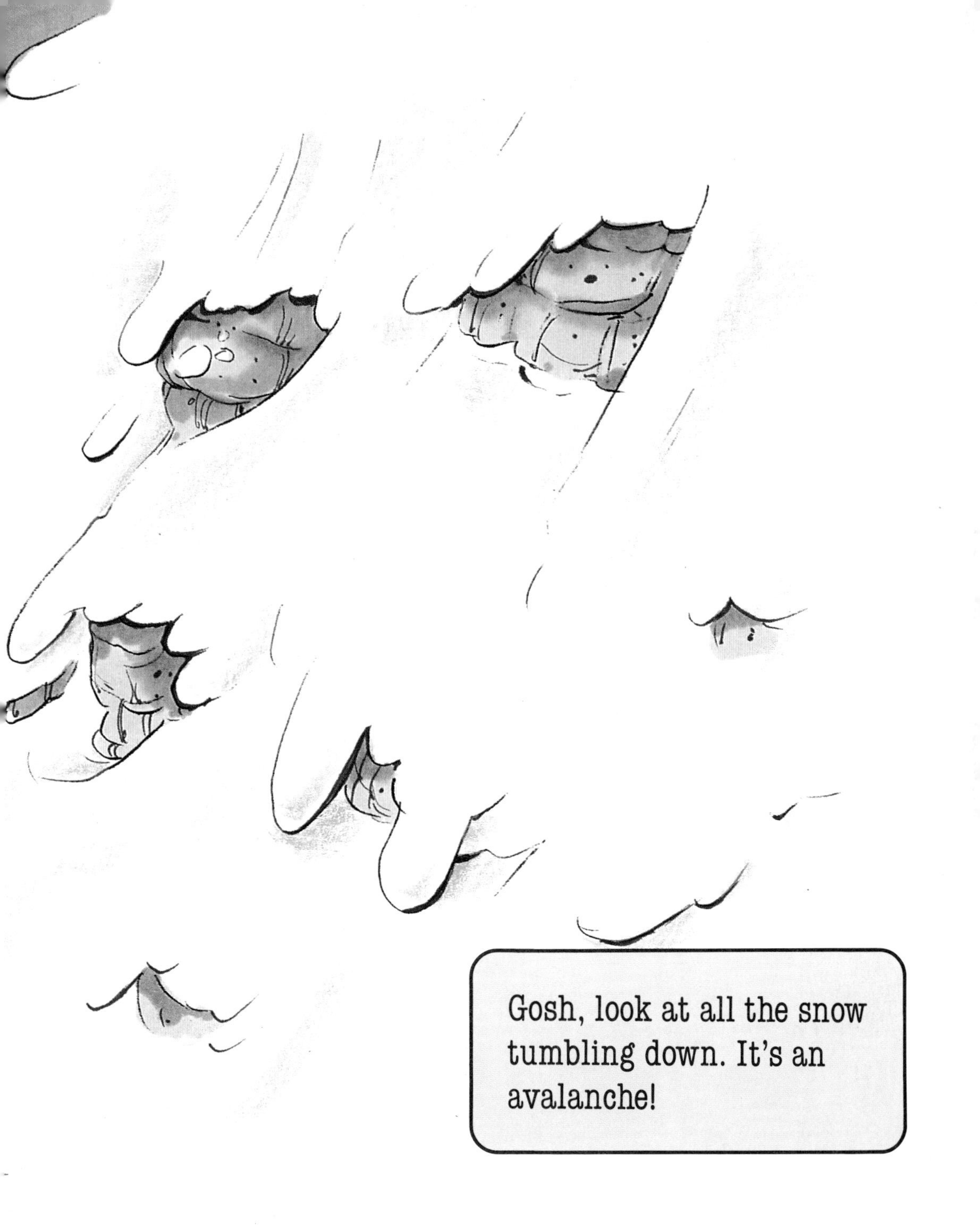
Gosh, look at all the snow tumbling down. It's an avalanche!

We decided to take Tweeg
some warm raisin muffins
and hot chocolate.

HARD TO FIND CITY
MOSS FOREST
KING NOGBURTS
WIZARD OF WEE GEE
GRUNGES
MUSHROOM FOREST
TREMBLY FAULT
THE GREAT DESERT
Land of GRUNDO